P9-BYU-681

THIS JUSTICE LEAGUE

COLLECTION BELONGS TO:

____

Dear Parent:
Your child's love of reading starts here!

Every child learns to read in a different way and at his or her own speed. Some go back and forth between reading levels and read favorite books again and again. Others read through each level in order. You can help your young reader improve and become more confident by encouraging his or her own interests and abilities. From books your child reads with you to the first books he or she reads alone, there are I Can Read Books for every stage of reading:

SHARED READING
Basic language, word repetition, and whimsical illustrations, ideal for sharing with your emergent reader

BEGINNING READING
Short sentences, familiar words, and simple concepts for children eager to read on their own

2 **READING WITH HELP**
Engaging stories, longer sentences, and language play for developing readers

3 **READING ALONE**
Complex plots, challenging vocabulary, and high-interest topics for the independent reader

ADVANCED READING
Short paragraphs, chapters, and exciting themes for the perfect bridge to chapter books

I Can Read Books have introduced children to the joy of reading since 1957. Featuring award-winning authors and illustrators and a fabulous cast of beloved characters, I Can Read Books set the standard for beginning readers.

A lifetime of discovery begins with the magical words **"I Can Read!"**

Visit www.icanread.com for information on enriching your child's reading experience.

I Can Read Book® is a trademark of HarperCollins Publishers.

3 IN 1: I CAN READ! JUSTICE LEAGUE COLLECTION
HARP40981

HARP40981

Manufactured in China.
This exclusive edition was printed for Kohl's Department Stores, Inc.
(for distribution on behalf of Kohl's Cares, LLC wholly owned) by HarperCollins Publishers.
For information address HarperCollins Children's Books, a division of
HarperCollins Publishers, 195 Broadway, New York, NY 10007.
www.icanread.com

ISBN: 978-0-06-285955-6

18 19 20 21 22 SCP 10 9 8 7 6 5 4 3 2 1

First Edition

Kohl's
Style number: 9780062859556
Factory Number 123386
05/2018

3 TREASURED STORYBOOKS for Young Readers!

JUSTICE LEAGUE

MEET THE JUSTICE LEAGUE

HARPER
An Imprint of HarperCollinsPublishers

TABLE OF CONTENTS

™

by Delphine Finnegan
pictures by Andie Tong

Batman created by Bob Kane with Bill Finger

My name is Bruce Wayne.
I live in Gotham City.
I own Wayne Enterprises.
We build the best high-tech gadgets.
We make everything from huge planes
to the smallest computers.

ENTERPRISES
WAYNE ENTERPRISES
BNDTS-1870

This work is important to me.
I drive the best cars.
I use the newest gadgets.
I need these tools
day *and* night.

When I get home,
I head to a secret cave.
It is deep underground.

I am Batman.

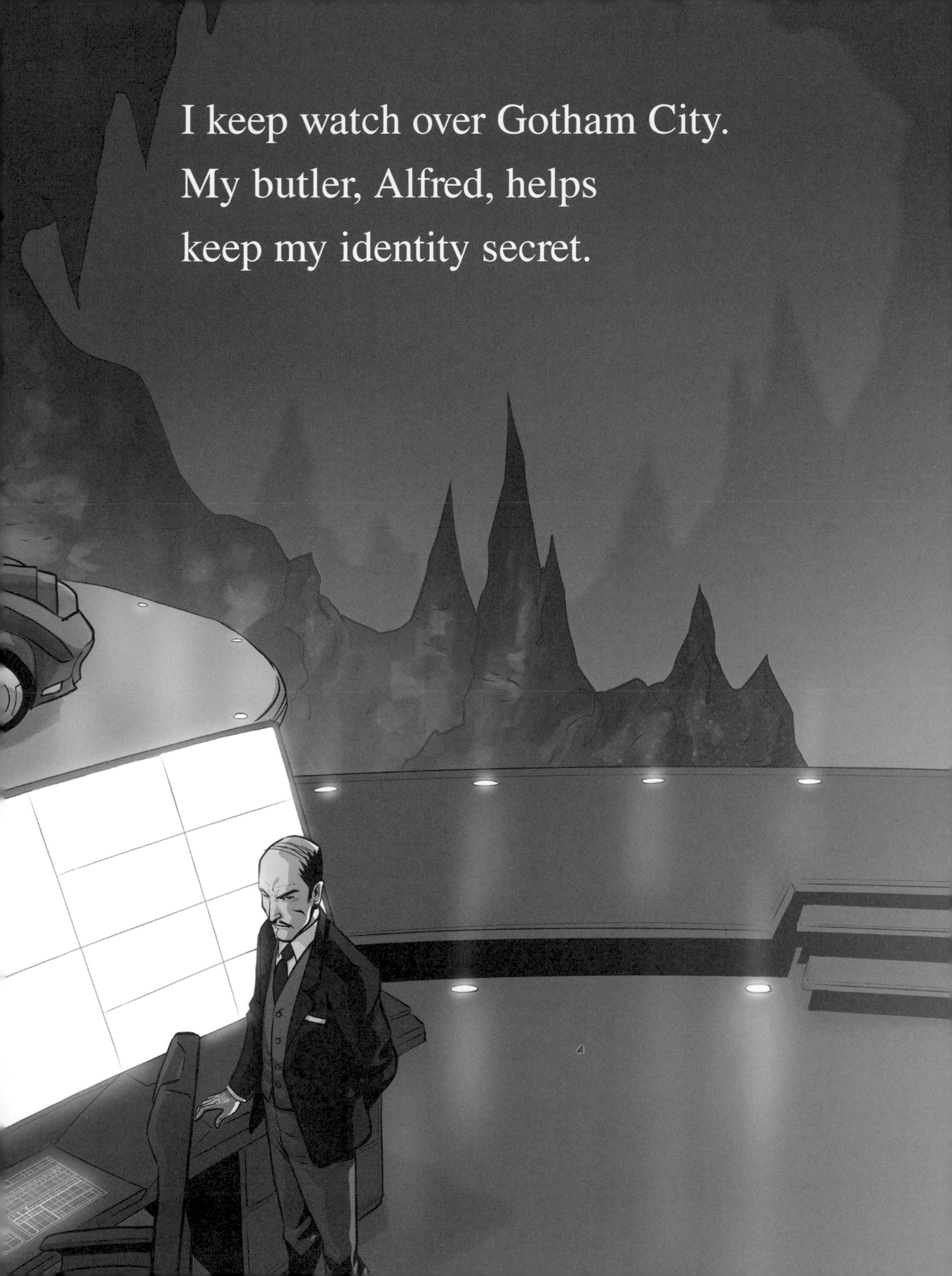

I keep watch over Gotham City.
My butler, Alfred, helps
keep my identity secret.

"Sir, you'll want to see this,"
says Alfred.
It is the Bat-Signal!
The Gotham City police send
this signal when they need my help.

My Batsuit and cape protect me.
My Utility Belt holds lots of gadgets.
I wear a mask
so no one knows who I am.

I jump into the Batmobile
and race into the night.

I contact Commissioner Gordon.
He is in charge
of Gotham City's police force.
"Something funny is happening
at the museum," he says.

When I arrive,
I see a poster about a new exhibit.
The rarest jewels
will be on display.
The show opens tomorrow.

I also see something strange.
The museum doors are wide open.
The alarm is broken.
All of the guards are gone.

I head to the main hall
and find the guards.
“This should do the trick,” I say.
Suddenly, a net falls down.
“Trick’s on you, Batman!”

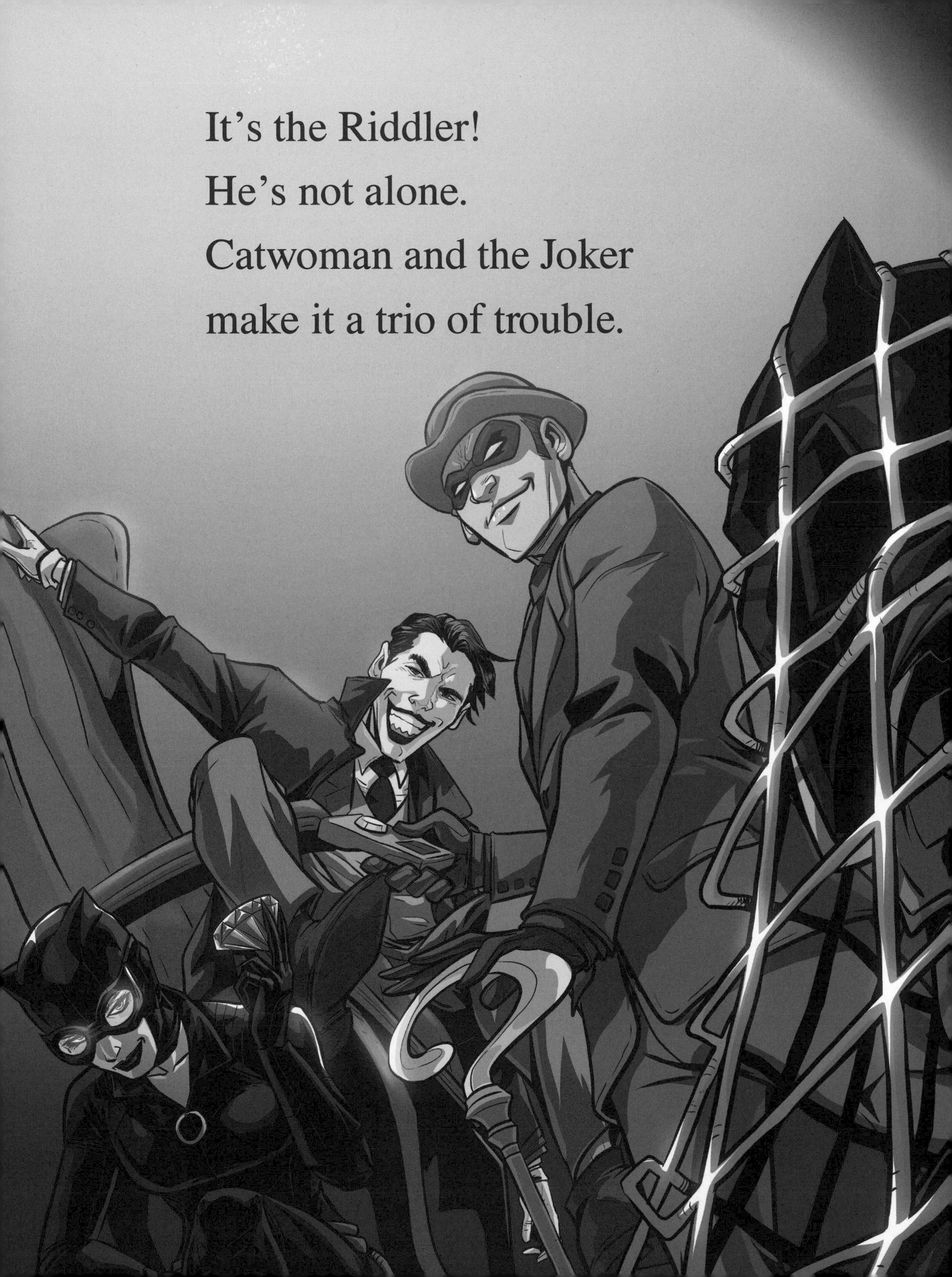

It’s the Riddler!
He’s not alone.
Catwoman and the Joker
make it a trio of trouble.

I twist and turn.
I try to get unstuck
from the net
while the three thieves
pack their bags.

I get free and grab my Batarangs.

Zip!

One slices the rope.

Zap!
I throw the other at the Riddler.
It stops him in his tracks.
But the Joker and Catwoman
get away.

"Call Commissioner Gordon.
Tell him I'll get this duo soon,"
I shout to the guards.
Then I follow the two fiends.

The Joker hitches a ride
from his crew.
Catwoman runs the other way.
"You have to pick a path,"
calls Catwoman.

I toss a tracer
at the Joker's helicopter.
It's a direct hit.

Then I follow Catwoman.
I chase her until
there is nowhere left to go.

Cats don't like water.

"You're cornered, Catwoman!"

I say.

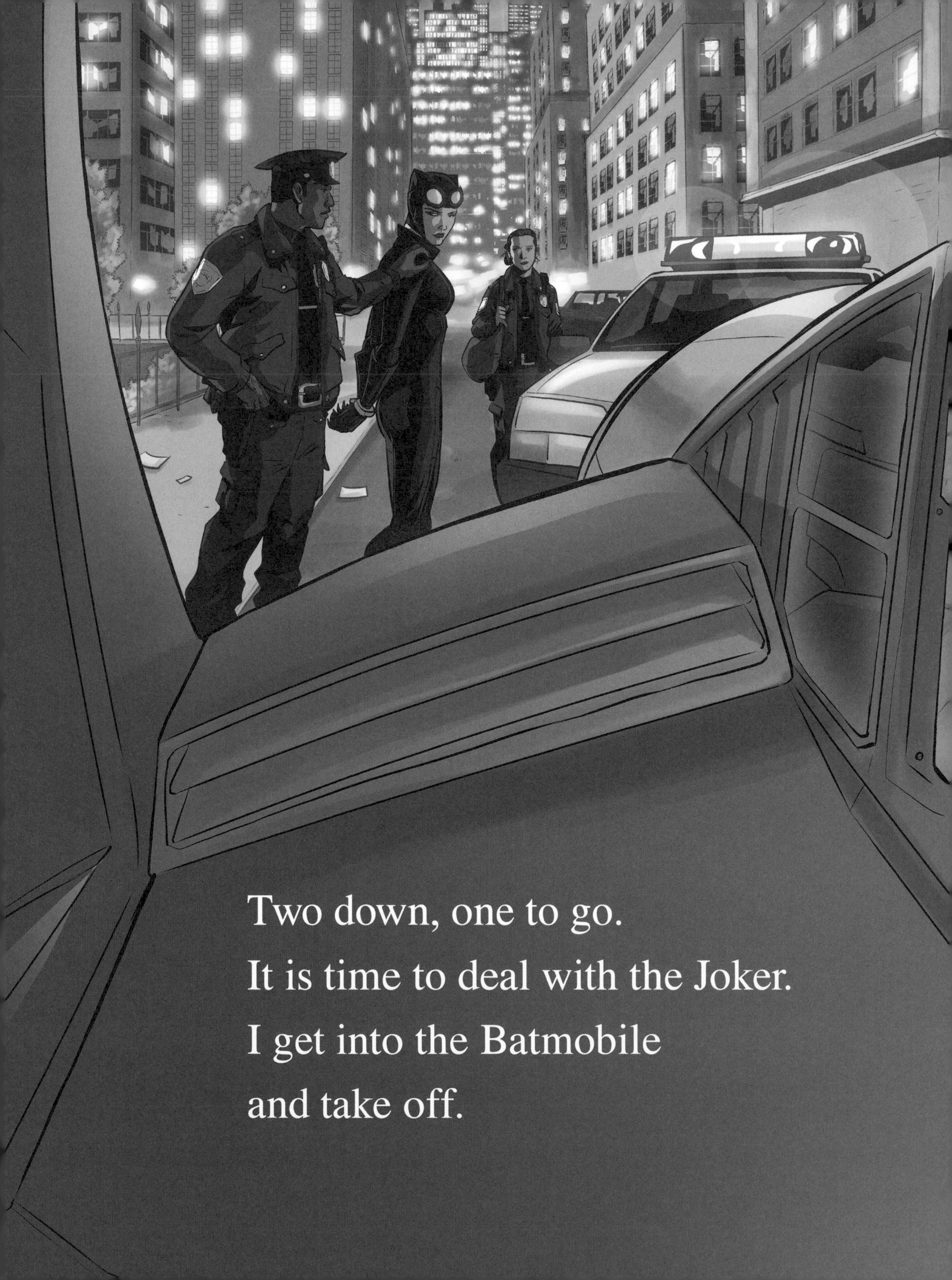

Two down, one to go.
It is time to deal with the Joker.
I get into the Batmobile
and take off.

I check the tracer.
It locates the Joker.
He is hiding in the hills.

The Joker throws a party
at his hilltop hideaway.
He shows his loot to his crew.
He tells joke after joke.
I wait for the right time to strike.

"Who invited this party crasher?" shouts the Joker.

"Time to tie up
some loose ends," I reply.

The Gotham City police arrive.
The trio of trouble
will be safely behind bars
and the jewels will return
to the museum.

I head out into the night.
Gotham City needs my help.
I will *always* answer the call.
I am Batman!

Meet the Justice League

by Lucy Rosen

pictures by Steven E. Gordon

colors by Eric A. Gordon

Today Clark Kent
was going to interview
the police chief of Metropolis.
But when Clark went to the station,
he knew something was wrong.
All the cops were standing still.
No one moved an inch.
A cop looked at Clark
with a strange, blank stare.

METROPOLIS POLICE
METROPOLIS POLICE
METROPOLIS POLICE

"I know that look," said Clark.
He turned the cop around.
There was a small starfish
stuck to the back of his neck!
Clark checked all the cops.
Everyone had a starfish!
"Starro!" he cried.

Clark knew he had to act.
"This looks like a job for Superman!"

Superman had faced Starro before.
The evil alien starfish
could take over anyone's mind.
He was a powerful enemy.
And this time, Starro had
even more people under control!

Superman needed help.
He called his friends
Batman and Wonder Woman.
But Starro had struck their cities, too!

“Starro cloned himself and sent his legion
to destroy our cities,” said Batman.
“To stop him, we’ll need help!”
Wonder Woman knew just who to call.
A few minutes later,
Superman, Batman, and Wonder Woman
were together with some new friends.

The Flash could run faster
than anyone on Earth.
Aquaman had the power
to swim deep into the ocean
without ever getting tired.
Martian Manhunter
could read people's thoughts.
And with his power ring,
Green Lantern could create
anything he could imagine.

"This is a big job," said Superman.
"We must defeat the clones,
then we have to find Starro
and stop him for good."

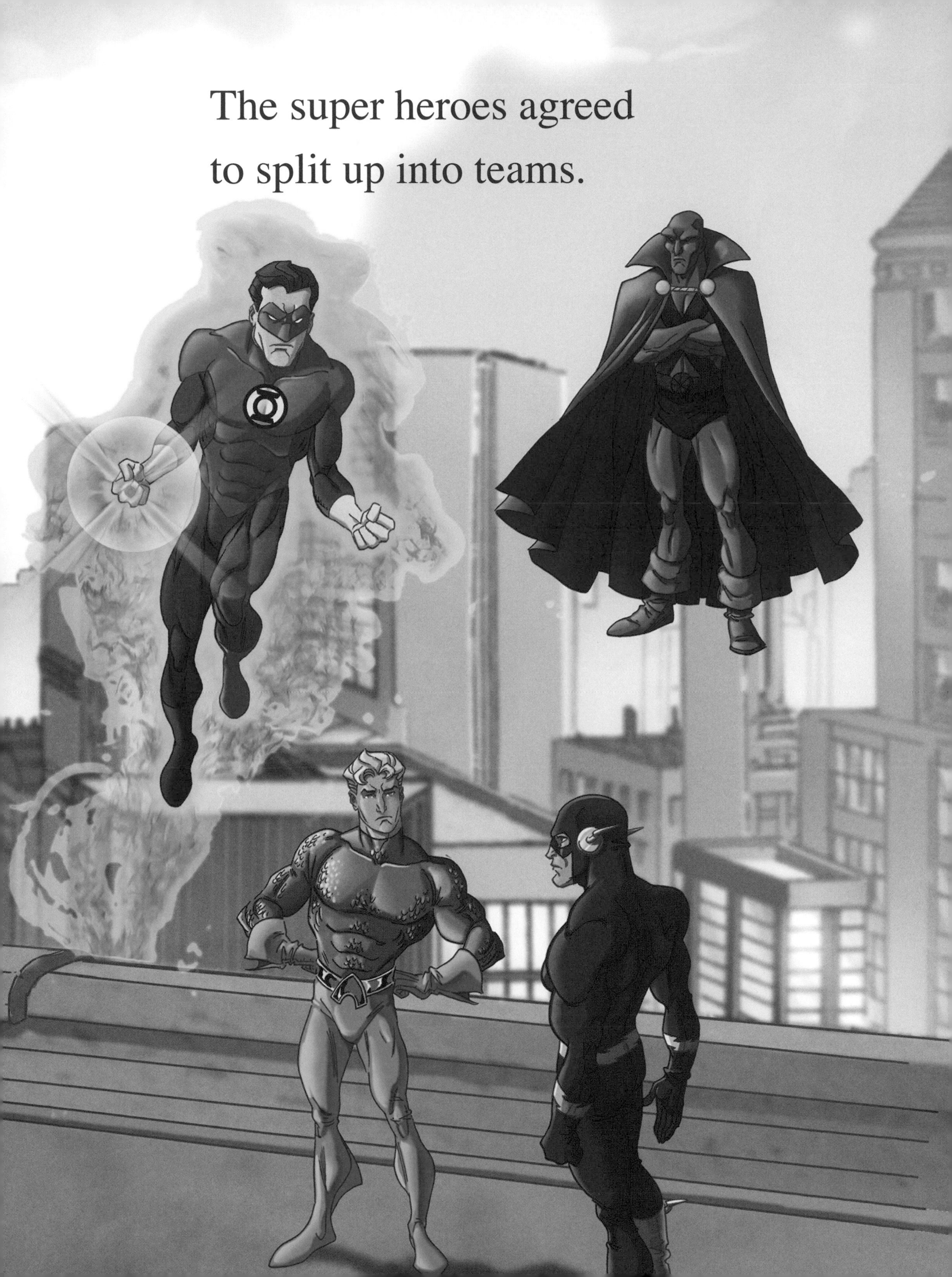

The super heroes agreed
to split up into teams.

Superman and the Flash
zoomed back to Metropolis.
The brainwashed cops
were all over the city!

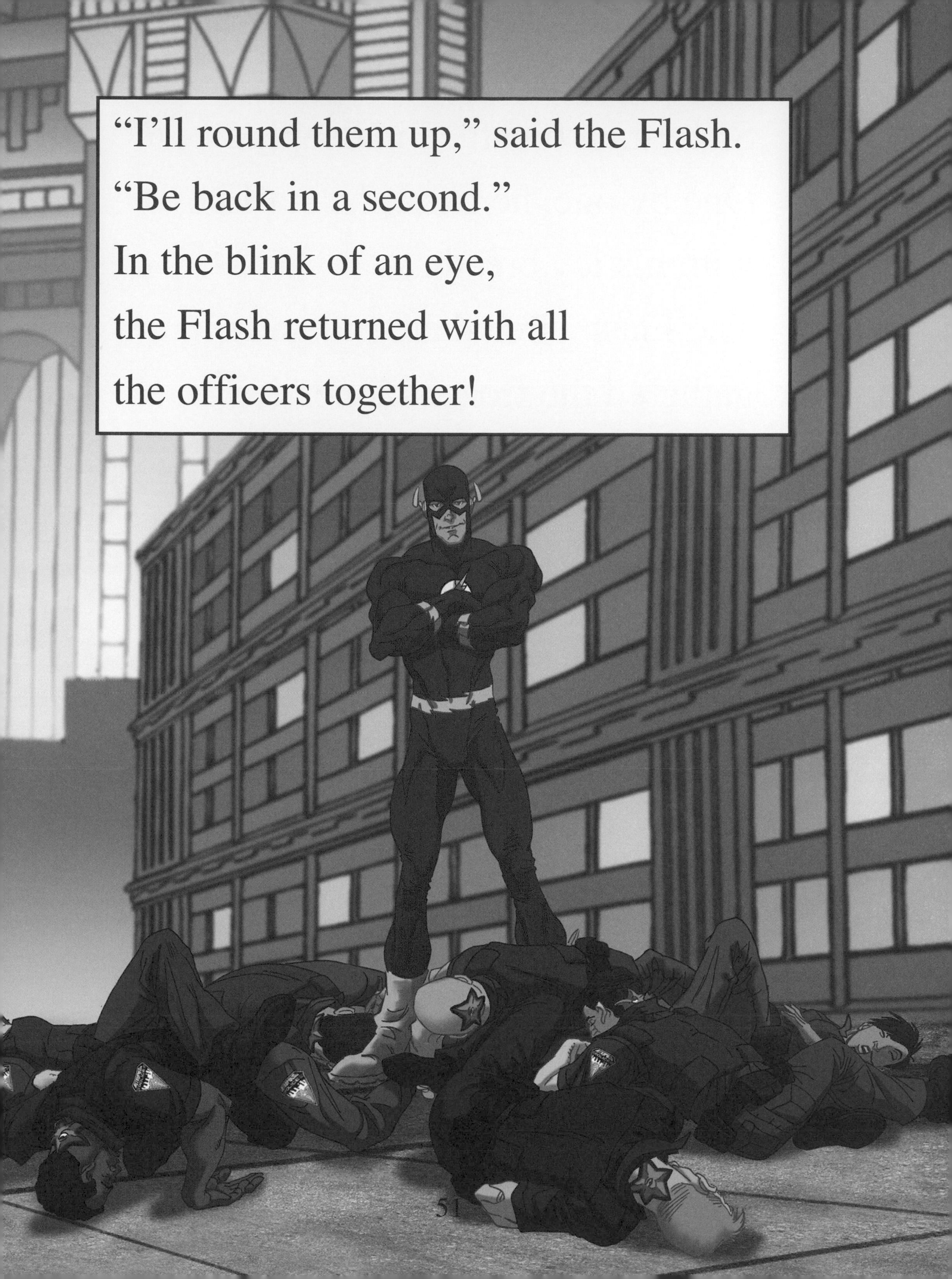
"I'll round them up," said the Flash.
"Be back in a second."
In the blink of an eye,
the Flash returned with all
the officers together!

Superman breathed in deeply.
One by one, he froze the starfish
with his icy breath.
The Flash circled around and
gathered the frozen clones.

“That was quick,”
the two speedy super heroes
laughed together.

The Flash and Superman raced to Gotham City. Batman had found all the clones with his Batcomputer. Between the Flash's speed, Superman's freeze breath, and Batman's combat skills, they had the clones collected in no time.

Meanwhile, in Washington, DC,
Green Lantern used his power ring
to find and gather the cops.
Wonder Woman snared one
in her Lasso of Truth.

"Tell me where Starro is,"
Wonder Woman said.
"He's in the depths of the sea,"
said the officer.

“We’ll see about that,”
said Wonder Woman.
“Martian Manhunter, do you copy?”
she said in her mind.

"Got it," said Martian Manhunter.
He and Wonder Woman
had linked minds.
"Time to hit the beach,"
the alien hero told Aquaman.

Martian Manhunter sent
the rest of the super heroes
a mental message.
They all met at the edge of the ocean.
Aquaman dived into the water.
He swam as fast as a shark.
There, in the murky depths
of the ocean,
he found the vile starfish.

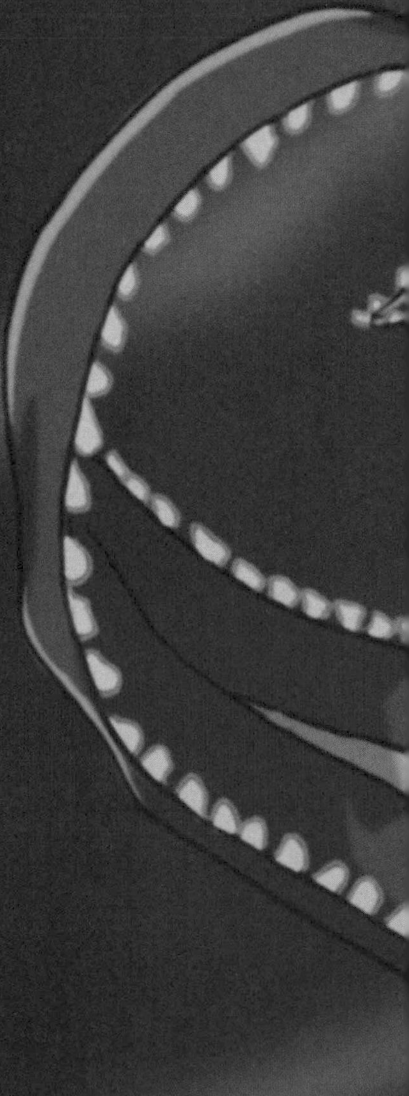

Aquaman grabbed Starro
by an arm and pulled him up.
Green Lantern used his ring
to help lift Starro out of the ocean.

Superman froze the villain with his icy breath.

“Time to get rid of this pest,”
said Martian Manhunter.
He and Superman
grabbed Starro and the clones
and flew them to outer space.
Superman used his super-breath
to scatter the starfish
all over the galaxy!

Back on Earth,
the super heroes celebrated.
"Nothing like teamwork to keep
the planet safe!" Batman said.

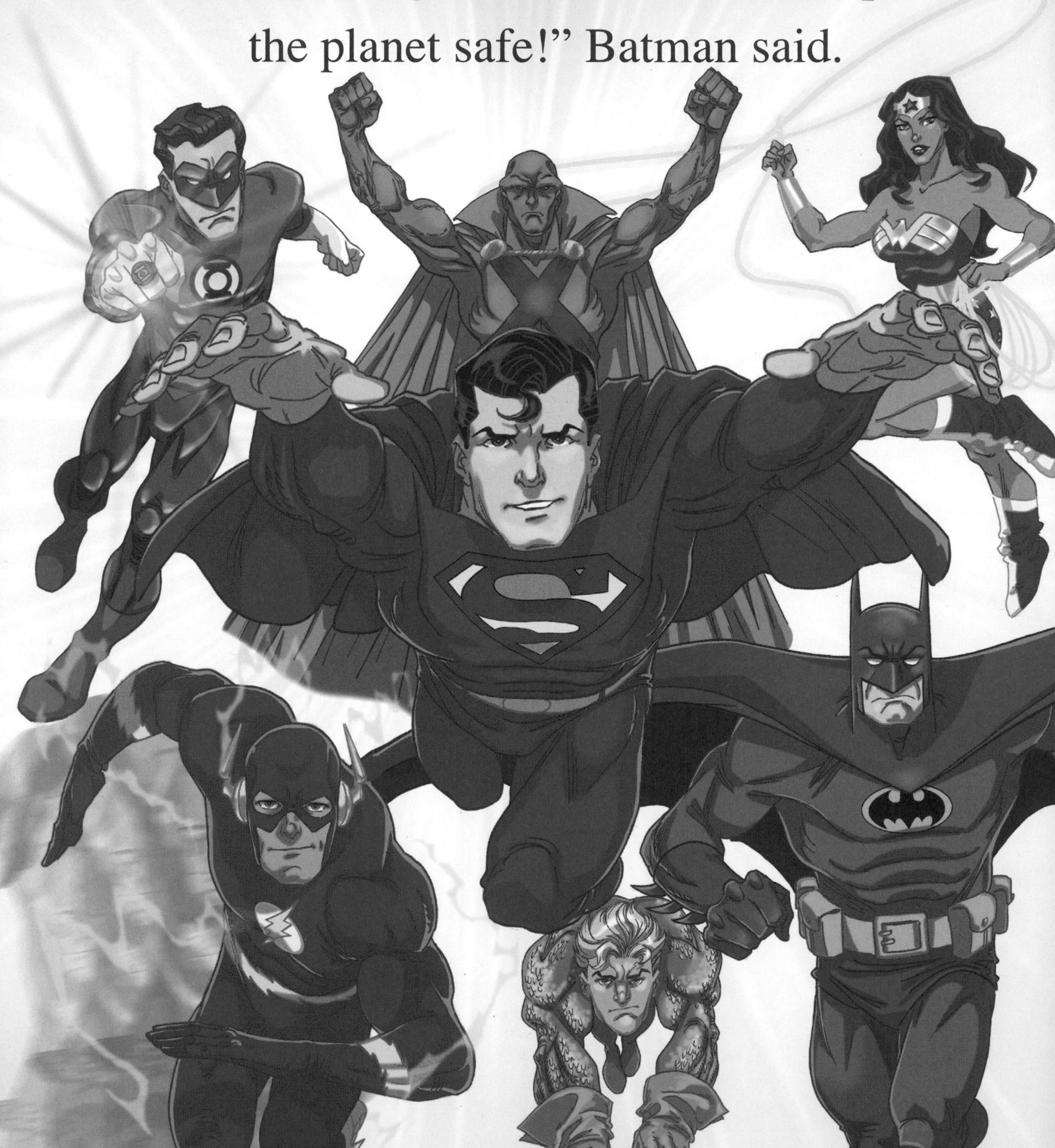

I Am Superman

by Michael Teitelbaum
pictures by Rick Farley

SUPERMAN created by Jerry Siegel and Joe Shuster
By special arrangement with the Jerry Siegel family

CLARK KENT

Clark Kent is a
newspaper reporter.
He is secretly Superman.

LOIS LANE

Lois Lane is a reporter.
She works for the
Daily Planet newspaper.

LEX LUTHOR

Lex Luthor is the
smartest criminal
in the world.
He is Superman's enemy.

THE FORTRESS OF SOLITUDE

This is Superman's
hidden home.
Many secrets about
his life are inside.

SUPERMAN

Superman has many amazing powers.
He was born on the planet Krypton.

Lois Lane sped past Clark Kent.
She was on her way out of
the Daily Planet,
where she and Clark worked.
They were newspaper reporters.

"Why are you in such a hurry, Lois?" asked Clark.

"I'm writing a story," Lois said.

"What kind of story?" Clark asked.

"That's my secret!" Lois said.

Lois rushed up to the roof.
Superman was waiting for her there.
"Hi, Lois," Superman said.
"Ready to do the story?"
"You bet, Superman!" Lois said.

"I thought we could talk somewhere a little different," Superman said.

"Where are we going?" Lois asked.

"You'll see," said Superman.

Superman flew at super-speed
up to the frozen Arctic.
“This is my Fortress of Solitude,”
Superman said.

"The Fortress is my secret home,"
he told Lois.
"If you want to learn about me,
this is the best place to come."

“This giant key unlocks the door,”
Superman said.
He put the key into the lock.
“I use my super-strength to lift it.”

Superman and Lois
entered the Fortress.
Superman used his super-breath
to blow the door closed.
"That's amazing!" said Lois.

Lois pointed at two statues.
“Who are those people?” she asked.
“Those are my parents,”
Superman said.
“My father, Jor-El,
and my mother, Lara.
They’re holding a model of Krypton.”
“Krypton?” Lois asked.

“Krypton was the planet
where I was born,” Superman said.
“This crystal shows pictures
of life on Krypton.”

“Krypton was different from Earth, but it was my home,” said Superman. “Then one day my father learned that Krypton was going to explode.”

"My father put me in a spaceship
and sent it to Earth
to save my life," Superman said.

"Earth's yellow sun gives me
my superpowers," said Superman.
"Even when I was a little boy,
I could lift a truck."

"Wow," said Lois.

"What else can you do?"

"I can see through things
with my X-ray vision," Superman said.

"And nothing can hurt me."

"Nothing?" Lois asked.

"Only kryptonite can make me weak,"
Superman said.
"It's a piece of my home planet.
I keep it in this case so it can't hurt me."

Suddenly, an alarm rang out.
Lex Luthor's angry face
filled up the computer screen.
"I will rule the city!" said Luthor.
"Watch what will happen
if I'm not given complete power!"

"Metropolis is in danger!" Superman said as he and Lois zoomed out of the Fortress. "I have to stop Luthor!"

Luthor blew up a building
as Superman and Lois arrived.
“The buildings are all empty,”
Superman said.
“At least no one got hurt.”

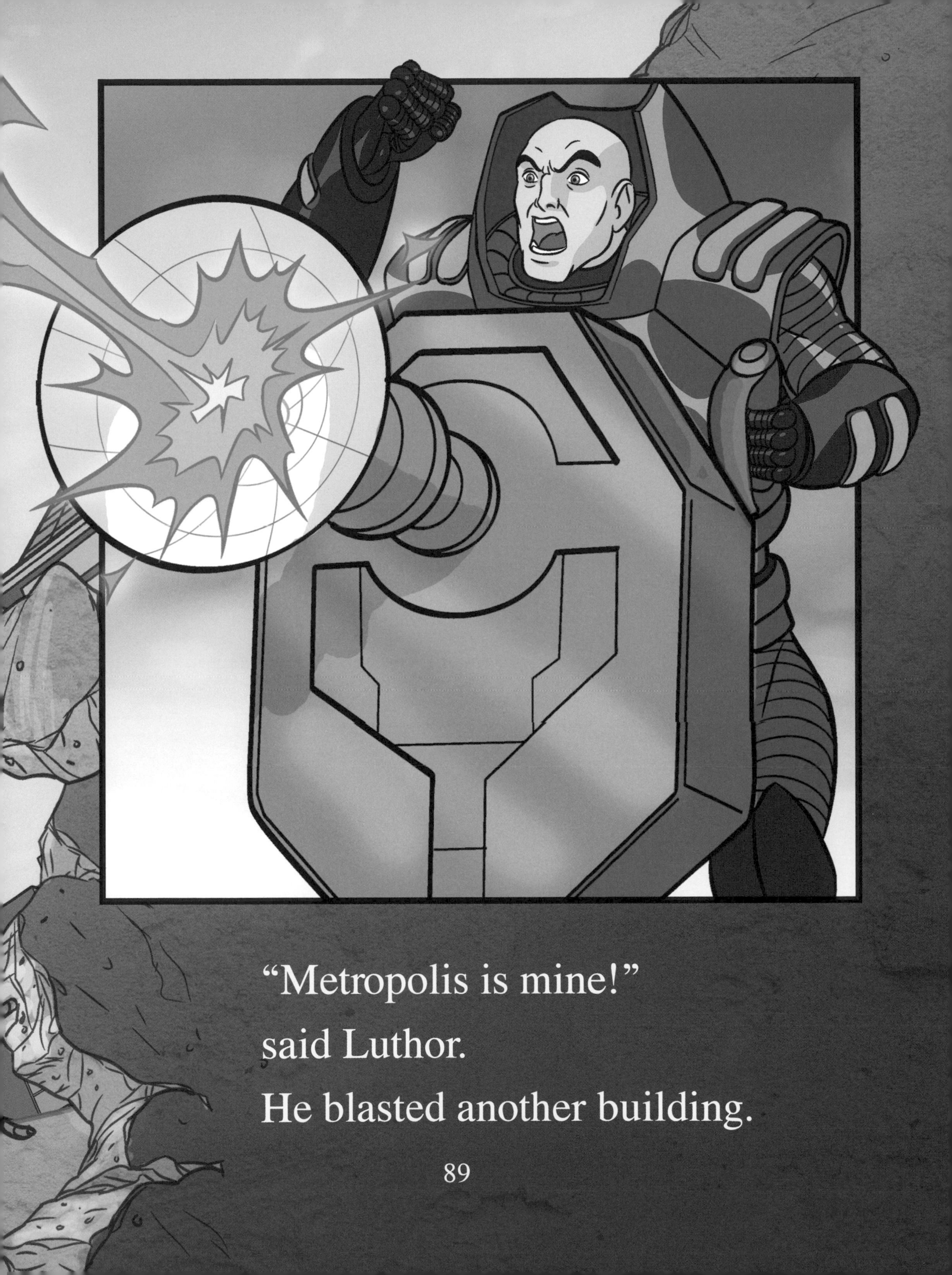

"Metropolis is mine!"
said Luthor.
He blasted another building.

A piece of stone fell toward Lois.
Superman soared up to catch it
and then tossed it
safely away.

"I can destroy Luthor's laser
with my heat vision," Superman said.
Two red beams shot out of his eyes.
Luthor's weapon blew up.

Superman stopped Luthor’s evil plot.
“Your days of making threats
are over!” he told the villain.
Superman gave Luthor to the police.

"Thanks for the story, Superman,"
Lois said when they returned to
the Daily Planet.
"I can't wait until Clark sees it!"
"Who's Clark?" Superman asked.
"Never mind!" Lois said.

The next day Lois hurried
into Clark's office.
She tossed a copy of
the Daily Planet onto his desk.

"Here's what I was doing
while you were just sitting around,"
Lois said to Clark.
"How do you do it?" Clark asked.
"That's my secret!" said Lois.

Lois walked out of Clark's office.
Clark smiled to himself.
"I have a secret, too," he said.
"I am Superman!"